Wiggens
Learns His Manners
At the Four Seasons Restaurant

LESLIE M^cGUIRK
and
ALEX von BIDDER

CANDLEWICK PRESS

Wiggens is a chocolate Labrador puppy and was a total rascal when it came to manners. His parents had tried to teach him how to behave, but Wiggens just couldn't seem to mind his manners!

Evidence of Bad Manners

yapping when you do not get what you want

chewing slippers

putting too much inside your mouth at one time

relieving yourself at the wrong time

rolling in something stinky

Wiggens's parents were almost ready to give up when they decided to seek help from the Chi-waa-waa, the oldest and wisest dog in Manhattan. Surely he would have suggestions on how to improve Wiggens's manners!

The Chi-waa-waa listened while Wiggens's parents told him about their son's behavior.

The Chi-waa-waa suggested that Wiggens's parents take their son to a very special and elegant place. He handed them a card. "This is a place where puppies can learn all the things they need to know about refinement and good manners," he said.

SHHH!

YAP
YAP
YAP

THE FOUR SEASONS
99 East 52nd Street
New York, NY 10022

Saint Bernard
Top Dog

The next day, Wiggens and his parents walked to the destination on the card — the Four Seasons Restaurant. His dad told him that dogs from all over the world come to practice their manners at the Four Seasons.

"They even have a special class for puppies like you," added his mom.

Wiggens felt very alone and small as he entered the lobby and climbed the stairs. "Hello there, pup," said the foxhound at the top. "The Saint Bernard has been waiting for you. Please wait here while I go and get him." Wiggens wagged his tail in reply.

Ode to the Bone

Zen Dog

He tried to wait patiently for the Saint Bernard, but it was hard to keep still. Wiggens squirmed and wiggled. He was excited and a little nervous too. With all his fidgeting, he didn't pay attention to a waiter walking by with a tray — oh, no!

WIGGENS'S LESSON #1

It is hard to control your excitement, but anytime you have to wait, it is better to sit still and not fidget. Waiting can get boring, so try to make a game of it — watch what's happening around you, and try to guess what will happen next!

When the Saint Bernard arrived, he shook Wiggens's paw. "Welcome! You must be a friend of the Chi-waa-waa. I've been looking forward to meeting you." Then he introduced Wiggens to the three other puppies in the class: Morgan, Tanker, and Fondue.

WIGGENS'S LESSON #2

When you meet someone, shake his or her paw and look him or her in the eye when you introduce yourself.

Wiggens and the other puppies followed the Saint Bernard as he led them into the large dining room. There was a pool right in the middle of it! Wiggens barked excitedly. He thought he was going to go swimming, which for a Labrador is a special treat — especially in the middle of Manhattan!

"No swimming today, Wiggens," the Saint Bernard told him. "We wouldn't want to disturb the other diners."

why does he wear a barrel?

He is a Saint Bernard. In the olden days, they rescued stranded skiers. The spirit of helping others is inside.

YAP

YAP

Wiggens and the other puppies sat down at a table next to the pool. The waiter came and gave them each a menu. Wiggens didn't know what to do with all the forks and spoons, and he didn't recognize anything on the menu!

Menu
* * *
Roasted Duck with Bing-Cherry Compote
*
Broiled Quail with Bacon and Oysters
*
Sirloin of Beef
*
Fetch of the Day
*
Assorted Biscuits

WIGGENS'S LESSON #4

When you don't know what to do, look at what others are doing. And don't be afraid to ask for help.

The puppies were scared to try some of the foods they had never heard of before. "Don't be afraid to taste new foods," said the Saint Bernard. "Just look at it as an adventure. You might find something you really like." And it was true. There were some foods they really, really liked, and others they definitely did not. The Saint Bernard told them it was OK if they didn't like something, as long as they tried it.

The Display of Weird Foods

After the puppies finished eating, the Saint Bernard took them into the kitchen to thank the chefs who had created their food. The puppies listened as the head chef told them about how their meal was prepared.

That pup is about to get in trouble!

While the chef was showing the puppies around the kitchen, Wiggens was more interested in a roasted duck on a plate nearby. When he thought no one was looking, he took it!

Wiggens, I know it is in
your nature to go after
ducks, but it's bad manners
to take something that
isn't yours.

WIGGENS'S LESSON #7

Always ask before you take something that doesn't
belong to you. Before you do something you shouldn't,
slow down and think before you act.

Wiggens felt very bad about taking the duck. To show how sorry he was, he offered to clean up the kitchen. The chef appreciated the help. The other three puppies offered to join in as well.

WIGGENS'S LESSON #8

Be sure to apologize when you do something
that is wrong, and see if there is anything
you can do to make it better.

When they returned to the dining room, the Saint Bernard asked, "Now would you like some dessert?"

"Yes, please," the puppies replied, wagging their tails. The Saint Bernard brought in a gigantic mound of Four Seasons cotton candy.

Wiggens even shared some with his parents, who had just arrived to pick him up. His parents thought that all the puppies seemed very well behaved. Wiggens had learned his manners!

WIGGENS'S LESSON #9

Don't forget to say "please" when you would like something, and remember, it is always fun to share.

As they were about to leave, the Saint Bernard presented the puppies with a small gift to remind them of their day at the Four Seasons. It was a small barrel, just like the one he wore. He explained that the spirit of good manners was inside each barrel.

"Remember," the Saint Bernard told them, "If you act with kindness and respect, you will always have good manners."

"Thank you, Saint Bernard," the puppies barked together.

WIGGENS'S LESSON #10

When someone has done something nice for you, say " Thank you" and show them you appreciate it.

For Alex, a magician with words and of life.
Thank you for believing that dogs in the restaurant made perfect sense.
L. M.

To Leslie, a friend who gets me.
Thank you for re-awakening and encouraging my creativity.
A. v. B.

Text copyright © 2009 by Leslie McGuirk and Alex von Bidder
Illustrations copyright © 2009 by Leslie McGuirk

The names "The Four Seasons" and "The Four Seasons Restaurant" as well as
the trademarked logo of the four trees are used by arrangement with
the Four Seasons Restaurant/Classic Restaurant Corporation.

First edition 2009

Library of Congress Cataloging-in-Publication Data is available.

Library of Congress Catalog Card Number 2008937596

ISBN 978-0-7636-4014-9

2 4 6 8 10 9 7 5 3 1

Printed in China

This book was typeset in Myriad Pro.
The illustrations were done in gouache.

Candlewick Press
99 Dover Street
Somerville, Massachusetts 02144

visit us at www.candlewick.com